Saved
at Sea

Saved at Sea

A Lighthouse Story

By
Mrs O F Walton

Christian Focus Publications

This edition © copyright 2002
Christian Focus Publications
Story written by O F Walton
Thinking Further Section
written by Catherine Mackenzie

Published by
Christian Focus Publications Ltd,
Geanies House, Fearn, Tain,
Ross-shire, IV20 1TW.
Scotland, Great Britain.

www.christianfocus.com
email: info@christianfocus.com

ISBN: 1-85792-795-8

Cover design by Catherine Mackenzie
Printed and bound by Cox and Wyman,
Cardiff Road, Reading.

An orphan boy who lives in a lighthouse, a ferocious storm, an amazing rescue, a happy reunion and a wonderful discovery - this story gripped me from the start.

Alick's life at the lighthouse is a roller coaster of loneliness, contentment, fear, joy, tragedy and love.

In the face of all these ups and downs, Alick and his grandfather, the lighthouse keeper, make the amazing discovery that Jesus is the Rock they can depend on whatever the future holds.

I hope this story will grip you, as it did me, and that it will challenge you about whether you can say along with Alick 'On Christ the solid rock I stand.'

Marina MacRae
Edinburgh, Scotland

•

Contents

My Strange Home 9

The Flare at Sea 19

The Bundle Saved 27

Little Timpey 39

The Unclaimed Sunbeam 49

The Old Gentleman's Question 59

A Thick Fog 69

Waiting for the Boat 77

A Change in the Lighthouse 87

Our New Neighbour 97

On the Rock 107

The Sunbeam Claimed 119

Thinking Further Section 130

My Strange Home

It was a strange day, the day that I was born. The waves were beating against the lighthouse, and the wind was roaring and raging against everything. Had not the lighthouse been built very firmly into the strong solid rock, it, and all within it, would have been swept into the deep wild sea.

It was a terrible storm. My grandfather said he had never known such a storm since he came to live on the island, more than forty years before.

Many ships went down in the storm that day, and many lives were lost. But in the very midst of it, when the wind was highest, and the waves were strongest, and when the foam and the spray had completely covered the lighthouse windows, I, Alick Ferguson, was born.

I was born on a strange day, and I was born into a strange home. The lighthouse stood on an island, four miles distant from any land. The island was not very large; if you stood in the middle of it you could see the sea all round you – that sea which was sometimes so blue and peaceful, and at other times was as black as ink, and roaring and thundering on the rocky shores of the little island. At one side of the island, on a steep rock overhanging the sea, stood the lighthouse. Night by night, as soon as it began to grow dark, the lighthouse lamps were lit.

I can remember how I used to admire those lights as a child. I would sit for hours watching them revolve and change in colour. First, there was a white light, then a blue one, then a red one, then a green one – then a white one again. And, as the ships went by, they always kept a lookout for our friendly lights, and avoided the rocks of which they warned.

My grandfather, old Sandy Ferguson, was

one of the lighthouse men, whose duty it was always to keep these lamps in order and to light them every night. He was a clever, active old man, and did his work well and cheerfully. His great desire was to be able to hold his post till I would be able to take his place.

At the time when my story begins I was nearly twelve years old, and daily growing taller and stronger. My grandfather was very proud of me, and said I should soon be a young man, and then he would get me appointed in his place to look after the lighthouse.

I was very fond of my strange home, and would not have changed it for any other. Many people would have thought it dull, for we seldom saw a strange face, and the lighthouse men were only allowed to go on shore for a few hours once in every two months. But I was very happy, and thought there was no place in the world like our little island.

Close to the tower of the lighthouse was

the house in which I and my grandfather lived. It was not a large house, but it was a very pleasant one. All the windows looked out to sea, and plenty of sharp sea air came in whenever they were opened. All the furniture in the house belonged to the lighthouse, and had been there long before my grandfather came to live there. Our cups and saucers and plates had the name of the lighthouse on them in large gilt letters, and a little picture of the lighthouse with the waves dashing round it. I used to think them very pretty when I was a boy.

We did not have many neighbours. There was only one other house on the island, and it was built on the other side of the lighthouse tower. The house belonged to Mr Millar, who shared the care of the lighthouse with my grandfather. Just outside the two houses was a courtyard, with a pump in the middle from which we got our water. There was a high wall all round this courtyard, to make a little shelter for us from the stormy wind.

Beyond this courtyard were two gardens,

divided by an iron railing. The Millars' garden was very untidy and forlorn, and filled with nettles, thistles, groundsel and all kinds of weeds, for Mr Millar had six little children and had no time to look after it.

But our garden was the admiration of everyone who visited the island. My grandfather and I were at work in it every fine day, and took pride in keeping it as neat as possible. Although it was so near the sea, our garden produced most beautiful vegetables and fruit, and the borders were filled with flowers, cabbage-roses, pansies, wallflowers and many other hardy plants, which were not afraid of the sea air.

Outside the garden was a good-sized field – full of small hillocks, over which the wild rabbits and hares, with which the island abounded, were continually scampering. In this field were kept a cow and two goats to supply the two families with milk and butter. Beyond it was the rocky shore and a little pier built out into the sea.

On this pier I used to stand every Monday morning to watch for the steamer, which called at the island once a week.

It was a great event for us when the steamer came. My grandfather and I and Mr and Mrs Millar and the children all came down to the shore to welcome it. This steamer brought our provisions for the week from a town some miles off, and often brought a letter for Mr Millar, or a newspaper for my grandfather.

My grandfather did not get many letters, for there were not many people that he knew. He had lived on that lonely island the greater part of his life and had been quite shut out from the world. All his relations were dead now, except my father, and what had become of him we did not know. I had never seen him, for he went away some time before I was born.

My father was a sailor, a fine, tall, strong young fellow, my grandfather used to say. He had brought my mother to the island and left her in my grandfather's care whilst he went on a voyage to Australia. He went from the island in that same little steamer which called every Monday morning. My grandfather stood on the end of the pier, as the steamer went out of sight, and my mother waved her handkerchief to him, as long as any smoke was seen on the horizon.

Grandfather has often told me how young and pretty she looked that summer morning. My father promised to write soon, but no letter came. Mother went down to the pier every Monday morning for three long years to see if it had brought her any word from her sailor husband.

But after a time her step became slower and her face paler, and at last she was too weak to go down the rocks to the pier when the steamer arrived on Monday morning. And soon after this I was left motherless.

From that day, the day on which my mother died, my grandfather became both father and mother to me. There was nothing he would not have

16

done for me, and wherever he went and whatever he did, I was always by his side.

As I grew older he taught me to read and write, for there was, of course, no school which I could attend. I also learnt to help him trim the lamps and to work in the garden. Our life went on very evenly from day to day, until I was about twelve years old. I used to wish sometimes that something new would happen to make a little change on the island.

And at last a change came.

The Flare at Sea

My grandfather and I were sitting at tea one dark November evening. We had been digging in the garden the whole morning, but in the afternoon it had become so wet and stormy that we had remained indoors.

We were sitting quietly at tea, planning what we would do the next day, when the door suddenly opened and Mr Millar put his head in.

"Sandy, quick!" he said. "Look here!"

My grandfather and I ran to the door and looked out over the sea. There, about three miles to the north of us, we saw a bright flare of light. It blazed up for a moment or two, lighting up the wild and stormy sea, and then it went out and all was darkness again.

"What is it, Grandfather?" I asked. But he did not answer me.

"There's no time to lose, Jem," he said; "out with the boat, my man!"

"It's an awful sea," said Millar, looking at the waves beating fiercely against the rocks.

"Never mind, Jem," said my grandfather, "we must do our best." So the two men went down to the shore and I followed them.

"What is it, Grandfather?" I asked again.

"There's something wrong out there," said he, pointing to the place where we had seen the light. "That's the flare they always make when they're in danger and want help at once."

"Are you going to them, Grandfather?"

"Yes, if we can get the boat out," he said. "Now, Jem, are you ready?"

"Let me go with you, Grandfather," I said,

"I might be able to help."

"All right, my lad," he said, "we'll try and see if we can get her off."

I can see that scene with my mind's eye, as though it were but yesterday. My grandfather and Mr Millar straining every nerve to row the boat from land, whilst I clung on to one of the seats, and tried in vain to steer her. I can see poor Mrs Millar standing on the pier with her shawl over her head, watching us, and two of her little girls clinging to her dress. I can see the waves, which seemed to be rising higher every moment and ready to beat our little boat to pieces. And I can see my grandfather's disappointed face, as, after many a fruitless attempt, he was obliged to give it up.

"It's no use, I'm afraid, Jem," he said at last, "we haven't hands enough to manage her."

So we got to shore as best we could, and paced up and down the little pier. We could see nothing more. It was a very dark night and all was perfect blackness over the sea.

The lighthouse lamps were burning brightly; they had been lit more than two hours before. It was Millar's turn to watch, so he went up to the tower, and my grandfather and I remained on the pier.

"Can nothing be done, Grandfather?"

"I'm afraid not, my lad; we can't make any headway against such a sea as this; if it goes down a bit we'll have another try at it."

But the sea did not go down. We walked up and down the pier almost in silence.

Presently a rocket shot up into the sky evidently from the same place where we had seen the flare.

"There she is again, Alick! Poor things! I wonder how many of them there are."

"Can we do nothing at all?" I asked again.

"No, my lad," he said, "the sea's too much for us. It's a terrible night. It puts me in mind of the day you were born."

So the night wore on. We never thought of going to bed, but walked up and down the pier with our eyes fixed on the place where we had seen the lights. Every now and then, for some hours, rockets were sent up; and then they ceased, and we saw nothing.

"They've got no more with them," said my grandfather. "Poor things! It's a terrible bad job."

"What's wrong with them, Grandfather?" I asked. "Are there rocks over there!"

"Yes, there's the Ainslie Crag just there; it's a nasty place that – a very nasty place. Many a fine ship has been lost there!"

At last the day dawned and a faint grey light spread over the sea. We could distinguish now the masts of a ship in the far distance. "There she is, poor thing!" said my grandfather, pointing in the direction of the ship. "She's close on Ainslie Crag – I thought so!"

"The wind's gone down a bit now, hasn't it?" I asked.

"Yes, and the sea's a bit stiller just now," he said. "Give Jem a call, Alick."

Jem Millar hastened down to the pier with his arms full of rope.

"All right, Jem, my lad," said my grandfather. "Let's be off; I think we may manage it now."

So we jumped into the boat and put off from the pier. It was a fearful struggle with the winds and waves. For a long time we seemed to make no way against them. Both the men were much exhausted and Jem Millar seemed ready to give in.

"Cheer up, Jem, my lad," said my grandfather, "think of all the poor fellows out there. Let's have one more try!"

So they made a mighty effort and the pier was left a little way behind. Slowly, very slowly, we made that distance greater; slowly, very slowly, Mrs Millar, who was standing on the shore, faded from our sight and the masts of the ship in distress seemed to grow a little nearer. Yet the waves were still fearfully strong and appeared ready, every moment, to

swallow up our little boat. Would my grandfather and Millar ever be able to hold on till they reached the ship, which was still more than two miles away?

"What's that?" I cried, as I caught sight of a dark object, rising and falling with the waves.

"It's a boat, surely!" said my grandfather. "Look, Jem!"

The Bundle Saved

It *was* a boat of which I had caught sight; a boat bottom upwards. A minute afterwards it swept close past us, so that we could almost touch it.

"They've lost their boat. Pull away, Jem!"

"Oh, grandfather!" I said; and the wind was so high, I could only make him hear by shouting, "Grandfather, do you think the boat was full?"

"No," he said. "I think they've tried to put her off and she's been swept away. Keep up, Jem!" For Jem Millar, who was not a strong man, seemed ready to give in.

We were now considerably more than halfway between the boat and the ship. It seemed as if those on board had caught sight of us, for another rocket went up. They had evidently kept one back, as a last hope, in case anyone should pass by.

As we drew nearer we could see that it was a large ship and we could distinguish many people moving about on deck.

"Poor fellows, poor fellows!" said my grandfather. "Pull away, Jem!"

Nearer and nearer we came to the ship, till at length we could see her quite distinctly. She had struck Ainslie Crag, and her stern was under water, and the waves were beating wildly on her deck. We could see

men clinging to the rigging that remained
and holding on to the broken masts of the
ship.

I shall *never* forget that sight to my dying
day! My grandfather and Jem Millar saw it,
and they pulled on desperately.

And now we were so near to the vessel, that had it not been for the storm, which was raging, we could have spoken to those on board. Again and again we tried to come alongside the shattered ship, but were swept away by the rush of the strong, relentless waves.

Several of the sailors came to the side of the ship and threw a rope out to us. It was long before we could catch it, but at last, as we were being carried past it, I clutched it and my grandfather immediately made it secure.

"Now!" he cried. "Steady, Jem! We shall save some of them yet!" and he pulled the boat as near as possible to the ship.

Oh! How my heart beat that moment, as I looked at the men and women all crowding towards the place where the rope was fastened.

"We can't take them all," said my grandfather, anxiously; "we must cut the rope when we've got as many as the boat will carry."

I shuddered, as I thought of those who would be left behind.

We had now come so close to the ship that the men on board would be able to wait their opportunity and jump into the boat whenever a great wave passed and there was lull for a moment in the storm.

"Look out, Jem!" cried my grandfather. "Here's the first."

A man was standing by the rope, with what appeared to be a bundle in his arms. The moment we came near he seized his opportunity and threw it to us. My grandfather caught it.

"It's a child, Alick!" he said; "put it down by you."

I put the bundle at my feet and my grandfather cried, "Now another; quick, my lads!"

But at this moment Jem Millar seized his arm. "Sandy! Look out!" he almost shrieked.

My grandfather turned round. A mighty wave, bigger than any I had seen before, was coming towards us. In another moment we should have been dashed, by its violence, against the ship and all have perished.

My grandfather hastily let go of the rope, and we just got out of the way of the ship before the wave reached us. And then came a noise, loud as a terrible thunderclap, as the mighty wave dashed against Ainslie Crag. I could hardly breathe, so dreadful was the moment.

O. F. Walton

"Now back for some more!" cried my grandfather, when the wave had passed.

We looked round, but the ship was gone! It had disappeared like a dream when one awakes, as if it had never been. That mighty wave had broken its back and shattered it into a thousand fragments. Nothing was to be seen of the ship or its crew, but a few floating pieces of timber!

My grandfather and Millar pulled hastily to the spot, but it was some time before we could reach it, for we had been carried by the sea almost a mile away and the storm seemed to be increasing in violence.

When at last we reached that terrible Ainslie Crag, we were too late to save a single life; we could not find one of those who had been on board. The greater number, no doubt, had been carried down in the vortex made by the sinking ship and the rest had risen and sunk again long before we reached them.

For some time we battled with the waves, unwilling to relinquish all hope of saving some of them. But we found at last that it was of no use and we were obliged to return. All had perished, except the child lying at my feet. I stooped down to it and could hear that it

was crying, but it was so tightly tied up in a blanket that I could not see it nor release it.

We had to strain every nerve to reach the lighthouse. It was not so hard returning as going, for the wind was in our favour, but the sea was still strong and we were often in great danger. I kept my eye fixed on the lighthouse lamps and steered the boat as straight as I could. Oh! How thankful we were to see those friendly lights growing nearer. And at last the pier came in sight, and Mrs Millar still standing there watching us.

"Have you got none of them?" she said, as we came up the steps.

"Nothing but a child," said my grandfather, sadly. "Only one small child, that's all. Well, we did our very best, Jem, me lad."

Jem was following my grandfather, with the oars over his shoulder. I came last, with that little bundle in my arms.

The child had stopped crying now and seemed to be asleep, it was so still. Mrs Millar wanted to take it from me and to undo the blanket, but my grandfather said, "Bide your time, Mary; bring the child into the house, my lass; it's bitter cold out here."

So we all went up through the field and through our garden and the courtyard. The blanket was tightly fastened round the child, except at the top, where room had been left for it to breathe, and I could just see a little nose and two closed eyes, as I peeped in at the opening.

The bundle was a good weight and before I reached the house I was glad of Mrs Millar's

help to carry it. We came into our little kitchen and Mrs Millar took the child on her knee and unfastened the blanket.

"Bless her," she said, as her tears fell fast, "it's a little girl!"

"Ay," said my grandfather, "so it is; it's a bonnie wee lassie!"

Little Timpey

I do not think I have ever seen a prettier face than that child's. She had light brown hair, round rosy cheeks and the bluest of blue eyes.

She awoke as we were looking at her, and seeing herself amongst strangers, she cried bitterly.

"Poor little thing!" said Mrs Millar. "She wants her mother."

"Ma-ma! Ma-ma!" cried the little girl, as she caught the word.

Mrs Millar fairly broke down at this and sobbed and cried as much as the child.

"Come, my lass," said her husband, "cheer up! Thee'll make her worse, if thee takes on so."

But Mrs Millar could do nothing but cry.

"Just think if it was our Polly," was all that she could say. "Oh, Jem, just think if it was our Polly that was calling for me!"

My grandfather took the child from her, and put her on my knee. "Now, Mary," he said, "get us a bit of fire and something to eat, there's a good woman! The child's cold and hungered, and we're much about the same ourselves."

Mrs Millar bustled about the house and soon lit a blazing fire; then she ran in next door to see if her children, whom she had left with a little servant girl, were all right, and she brought back with her some cold meat for our breakfast.

I sat down on a stool before the fire, with the child on my knee. She seemed to be about two years old, a strong healthy little thing. She had stopped crying now and did not seem to be afraid of me; but whenever any of the others came near she hid her face in my shoulder.

Mrs Millar brought her a bowl of bread and milk, and she let me feed her.

She seemed very weary and sleepy, as if she could hardly keep her eyes open. "Poor wee lassie!" said my grandfather, "I expect they pulled her out of bed to bring her on deck. Won't you put her to bed?"

"Yes," said Mrs Millar, "I'll put her in our Polly's bed; she'll sleep there quite nicely, she will."

But the child clung to me, and cried so loudly when Mrs Millar tried to take her, that my grandfather said, "I wouldn't take her away, poor motherless lamb; she takes kindly to Alick; let her bide here." So we made a bed for her on the sofa and Mrs Millar brought one of little Polly's nightgowns and undressed and washed her, and put her to bed.

The child was still very shy of all of them but me. She seemed to have taken to me from the first and when she was put into her little bed she held out her tiny hand to me, and said: "Handie, Timpey's handie."

"What does she say? Bless her!" said Mrs Millar, for it was almost the first time that the child had spoken.

"She wants me to hold her hand," I said, "Timpey's little hand. Timpey must be her name!"

"I never heard of such a name," said Mrs Millar. "Timpey, did you say?"

"What do they call you, darling?" she said to the child.

But the little blue eyes were closing wearily and very soon the child was asleep. I still held that tiny hand in mine as I sat beside her; I was afraid of waking her by putting it down.

"I wonder who she is?" said Mrs Millar, in a whisper, as she folded up her little clothes. "She has beautiful things on, to be sure! She has been well taken care of, anyhow! Stop, here's something written on the little petticoat; can you make it out, Alick?"

I laid down the little hand very carefully, and took the tiny petticoat to the window.

"Yes," I said, "this will be her name. Here's *Villiers* written on it."

"Dear me!" said Mrs Millar. "Yes, that will be her name! Dear me, dear me, to think of her poor father and mother at the bottom of that dreadful sea! Just think if it was our Polly!" And then Mrs Millar cried so much again that she was obliged to go home and finish her cry, with little Polly clasped tightly in her arms.

My grandfather was worn out with all he had done during the night, and went upstairs to bed. I sat watching the little sleeping child. I felt as if I could not leave her.

She slept very quietly and peacefully. "Poor little pet, how little she knows what has happened," I thought; and my tears came fast and fell on the little hand which was lying on the pillow. But after a few minutes I leaned my head against the sofa and fell fast asleep. I had had no sleep the night before and was quite worn out.

I was awakened, some hours after, by some one pulling my hair and a little voice calling in my ear, "Up! Up boy! Up! Up!"

I looked up and saw a little roguish face looking at me; the merriest, brightest little face you can imagine.

"Up, up, boy, please!" she said again, in a coaxing voice.

So I lifted up my head and she climbed out of her little bed on the sofa on to my knee.

"Put shoes on, boy," she said, holding out her little bare toes.

I put on her shoes and stockings and then Mrs Millar came in and dressed her.

It was a lovely afternoon; the storm had ceased whilst we had been asleep and the sun was shining brightly. I got the dinner ready and the child watched me and ran backwards and forwards, up and down the kitchen. She seemed quite at home now and very happy.

My grandfather was still asleep, so I did not wake him. Mrs Millar brought in some broth she had made for the child and we dined together. I wanted to feed her as I had done the night before, but she said, "Timpey have *poon*, please!" and took the spoon from me and fed herself so prettily, I could not help watching her.

"God bless her, poor little thing!" said Mrs Millar.

"God bless *ou*," said the child; the words were evidently familiar to her.

"She must have heard her mother say so," said Mrs Millar, in a choking voice.

When we had finished dinner, the child slipped down from her stool and ran to the sofa. Here she found my grandfather's hat, which she put on her head, and my scarf, which she hung round her neck. Then she marched to the door and said, "Tatta, tatta; Timpey go tatta."

"Take her out for a bit, Alick," said Mrs Millar. "Stop a minute, though, I'll fetch our Polly's hood." So, to her great delight, we dressed her in Polly's hood and put a warm shawl round her and I took her out.

Oh! How she ran and jumped and played in the garden. I never saw such a merry little thing, picking up stones, gathering daisies ("*day-days*" she called them), running down the path and calling to me to catch her. She was never still for an instant!

But every now and then, as I was playing with her, I looked across the sea to Ainslie Crag. The sea had not gone down much, though the wind had ceased, and I saw the waves still dashing wildly upon the rocks. And I thought of what lay beneath them, of

the shattered ship, and of the child's mother. "Oh! If she only knew," I thought, as I listened to her merry laugh which made me more ready to cry than her tears had done.

The Unclaimed Sunbeam

My grandfather and Jem Millar were sitting over the fire in the little watch-room in the lighthouse tower and I sat beside them with the child on my knee. I had found an old picture book for her and she was turning over the pages and making her funny little remarks about the pictures.

"Well, Sandy," said Millar, "what shall we do with her?"

"Do with her?" said my grandfather, stroking her little fair head. "We'll keep her! Won't we, little lassie?"

"Yes," said the child, looking up and nodding her head, as if she understood all about it.

"We ought to look up some of her relations, it seems to me," said Jem. "She's sure to have some, somewhere."

"And how are we to find them out?" asked my grandfather.

"Oh, the captain can soon find out for us what ship is missing, and we can send a line to the owners; they'll know who the passengers were."

"Well," said my grandfather, "maybe you're right, Jem, we'll see what they say. But for my part, if them that cares for the child is at the bottom of the sea, I hope no one else will come and take her away from us."

"If I hadn't so many of them at home..." began Millar.

"Oh yes my lad, I know that," said my grandfather, interrupting him, "but thy house is full enough already. Let the wee lassie come to Alick and me. She'll be a nice little bit of company for us; and Mary will see to her clothes and such like, I know."

"Yes, that she will," said her husband. "She has been crying about that child the best part of the day! She has indeed!"

My grandfather followed Jem's advice and told Captain Sayers when he came in the steamer the next Monday, the whole story of the shipwreck, and asked him to find out the name and address of the owners of the vessel.

I hoped that no one would come to claim my little darling. She became dearer to me every day and I felt as if it would break my heart to part with her. Every night when Mrs Millar had undressed her, she knelt beside me in her little white nightgown to "talk to God," as she called praying. She had evidently learnt a little prayer from her mother, for the first night she began of her own accord.

"Jesus, Eppy, hear me."

I could not think at first what it was that she was saying; but Mrs Millar said she had learnt the hymn when she was a little girl, and she wrote out the first verse for me. Every night afterwards I let the child repeat it after me.

"Jesus, tender Shepherd, hear me,
Bless Thy little lamb tonight,
Through the darkness
be Thou near me,
Keep me safe till morning light."

I thought I should like her always to say the prayer her mother had taught her. I never prayed myself – my grandfather had never taught me. I wondered if my mother would have taught me if she had lived. I thought she would.

I knew very little, in those days, of the Bible. My grandfather did not care for it and never read it. He had a large Bible, but it was always laid on the top of the chest of drawers as a kind of ornament; and unless I took it down to look at the curious old pictures inside, it was never opened.

Sunday on the island was just the same as any other day. My grandfather worked in

52

the garden or read the newspaper, just the same as usual, and I rambled about the rocks or did my lessons, or worked in the house, as I did every other day in the week. We had no church or chapel to go to, and nothing happened to mark the day.

I often think now of that dreadful morning, when we went across the stormy sea to that sinking ship. If our boat had capsized then, if we had been lost, what would have become of our souls? It is a very solemn thought, and I cannot be too thankful to God for sparing us both a little longer. My grandfather was a kind-hearted, good-tempered, honest old man, but I know now that that is not enough to open the door of heaven. Jesus is the only way there, and my grandfather knew little of and cared nothing for *Him*.

Little Timpey became my constant companion, indoors and out of doors. She was rather shy of the little Millars, for they were noisy and rough in their play, but she clung to me, and never wanted to leave me. Day by day she learnt new words and came out with such odd little remarks of her own, that she made us all laugh. Her great pleasure was to get hold of a book and pick out the different letters of the alphabet, which, although she could hardly talk, she knew quite perfectly.

Dear little pet! I can see her now, sitting at my feet on a large flat rock by the seashore, and calling me every minute to look at A, or B, or D, or S. And so by her pretty ways she crept into all our hearts, and we quite dreaded the answer coming to the letter my grandfather had written to the owners of *The Victory*, which, we found, was the name of the lost ship.

It was a very wet day, the Monday that the answer came. I had been waiting some time on the pier and was wet through before the steamer arrived. Captain Sayers handed me the letter before anything else and I ran up with it to my grandfather at once. I could not wait until our provisions and supplies were brought on shore.

Little Timpey was sitting on a stool at my grandfather's feet, winding a long piece of tape round and round her little finger. She ran to meet me as I came in, and held up her face to be kissed.

What if this letter should say she was to leave us and go back by the steamer! I drew a long breath as my grandfather opened it.

It was a very civil letter from the owners of the ship, thanking us for all we had done to try to save the unhappy crew and passengers, but saying they knew nothing of the child or her belongings, as no one by

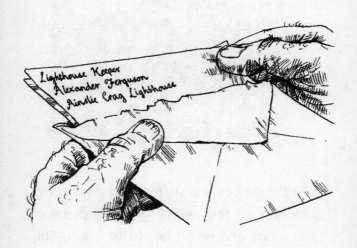

Lighthouse Keeper
Alexander Ferguson
Ainslie Crag Lighthouse

the name of Villiers had taken a cabin and there was no sailor on board of that name. But they said they could make further enquiries in Calcutta, from which port the vessel had sailed. Meanwhile, they begged my grandfather to take charge of the child and assured him he should be handsomely rewarded for his trouble.

"That's all right!" I said, when he had finished reading it. "Then she hasn't to go yet!"

"No," said my grandfather, "poor wee lassie, we can't spare her yet. I don't want any of their rewards, Alick, not I! That's reward enough for me," he said, as he lifted the child up to kiss his wrinkled forehead.

The Old Gentleman's Question

The next Monday morning Timpey and I went down together to the pier, to await the arrival of the steamer. She had brought a doll with her, which Mrs Millar had given her and of which she was very proud. Captain Sayers sent for me, as soon as the steamer came up to the pier, to tell me that two gentlemen had come to see my grandfather. I held the child's hand very tightly in mine, for I felt sure they had come for her.

The gentlemen came up the steps a minute or two afterwards. One of them was a middle-aged man, with a very clever face, I thought. He told me that he had come to see Mr Alexander Ferguson, and asked me if I could direct him which way to go to the house.

"Yes, sir," I said. "Mr Ferguson is my grandfather." So we went up towards the lighthouse, Timpey and I walking first to lead the way, and the gentlemen following. The other gentleman was quite old and had white hair and gold spectacles and a pleasant kindly face.

Timpey could not walk very fast and she kept running first to one side and then to another, to gather flowers or pick up stones, so I took her in my arms and carried her.

"Is that your little sister?" asked the old gentleman.

"No, sir," I said, "this is the little girl who was on board the *Victory*."

"Dear me! Dear me!" said both gentlemen at once. "Let me look at her," said the old man, arranging his spectacles.

But Timpey was frightened, and clung to me and began to cry. "Never mind, never mind," said the old gentleman, kindly, "we'll make friends with one another by-and-by."

By this time we had reached the house, and the middle-aged gentleman introduced himself as Mr Septimus Forster, one of the owners of the lost vessel, and said that he and his father-in-law, Mr Davis, had come to hear all particulars that my grandfather could give them with regard to the shipwreck.

My grandfather begged them to sit down, and told me to prepare breakfast for them at once. They were very pleasant gentlemen, both of them, and were very kind to my grandfather. Mr Forster wanted to make him a handsome present for what he had done; but my grandfather would not take it. They talked much of little Timpey, and I kept stopping to listen as I was setting out the cups and saucers. They had heard nothing more of her relations, and they said it was a very strange thing that no such name as Villiers was to be found on the list of passengers on board. They offered to take her away with them till some relation was found, but my grandfather begged to keep her. The gentlemen, seeing how happy and well cared for the child was, gladly consented.

After breakfast Mr Forster said he should like to see the lighthouse, so my grandfather went up to the top of the tower with him and showed him, with great pride, all that was to be seen there. Old Mr Davis was tired and stayed behind with little Timpey and me.

"This is a strong house, my lad," he said, when the others had gone.

"Yes, sir," I said, "it ought to be strong; the wind is fearful here sometimes."

"What sort of foundation has it?" said the old man, tapping the floor with his stick.

O. F. Walton

"Oh, it's solid rock, sir," I answered, "solid rock; our house and the lighthouse tower are all built into the rock, they would never stand if they weren't."

"And are *you* on the rock, my lad?" said Mr Davis, looking at me through his spectacles.

"I beg your pardon, sir," I said, for I thought I had not heard him rightly.

"Are *you* on the rock?" he repeated.

"On the rock, sir? Oh yes," I said, thinking he could not have understood what I said before. "All these buildings are built into the rock or the wind and sea would carry them away."

"But *you*," said the old gentleman, again, "are *you* on the rock?"

"I don't quite understand you, sir," I said.

"Never mind," he said, "I'll ask your grandfather when he comes down." So I sat still, wondering what he could mean, and almost thinking he must have gone out of his mind.

As soon as my grandfather returned, he

put the same question to him, and my grandfather answered it as I had done, by assuring him how firmly and strongly the lighthouse and its surroundings were built into the solid rock.

"And you yourself?" said Mr Davis, "How long have you been on the rock?"

"I, sir?" said my grandfather. "I suppose you mean how long have I lived here; forty years, sir – forty years come the twelfth of next month I've lived on this rock."

"And how much longer do you expect to live here?" said the old gentleman.

"Oh, I don't know, sir," said my grandfather. "As long as I live, I suppose. Alick, here, will take my place by-and-by; he's a fine strong boy is Alick, sir."

"And where will you live when you leave the island?" asked Mr Davis.

"Oh, I never mean to leave it," said my grandfather, "not till I die, sir."

"And *then*; where will you live *then*?"

"Oh, I don't know, sir," said my grandfather. "In heaven, I suppose. But, dear me, I'm not going there just yet," he said, as if he did not like the turn the conversation was taking.

"Would you mind answering me one more question?" said old Mr Davis. "Would you kindly tell me *why* you think you'll go to heaven? You won't mind me asking you, will you?"

"Oh dear, no," said my grandfather, "not at all, sir. Well, you see I've never done anybody any harm, and God is very merciful, and so, I've no doubt it will be all right at last."

"Why, my dear friend," said the old gentleman, "I thought you said you were on the rock. You're not on the rock at all, you're on the sand!" He was going to add more, when one of Captain Sayers' men ran up to say the steamer was ready to start, and would they kindly come at once, as it was late already. So the two gentlemen jumped up and prepared hastily to go down to the beach.

But as old Mr Davis took leave of my grandfather, he said, earnestly:

"My friend, you are building on the sand; you are indeed, and it won't stand the storm, no, it won't stand the storm!" He had no time to say more; the sailor hastened him away.

I followed them down to the pier and stood there watching the steamer preparing to start.

There was a little delay after the gentlemen went on board, and I saw Mr Davis sit down on a seat on deck, take out his pocket book, and write something on one of the leaves. Then he tore the leaf out, and gave it to one of the sailors to hand to me as I stood on the pier and in another moment the steamer had started.

A Thick Fog

That little piece of paper, which was given to me that day, I have it still, put amongst my greatest treasures. There was not much written on it, only two lines of a hymn:

"On Christ, the solid Rock, I stand,
   All other ground is sinking sand."

I walked slowly up to the house, thinking. My grandfather was out with Jem Millar, so I did not show him the paper then, but I read the lines many times over as I was playing with little Timpey, and I wondered very much what they meant.

In the evening, my grandfather and Jem Millar generally sat together over the fire in the little watch-room upstairs, and I used to take little Timpey up there, until it was time for her to go to bed. She liked climbing up the stone steps in the lighthouse tower. She used to call out, "Up! Up! Up!" as she went along, until she reached the top step, and then she would run into the watch-room with a merry laugh.

As we went in, that evening, my grandfather and Jem were talking together of the visit of the two gentlemen. "I can't think what the old man meant about the rock," my grandfather was saying. "I couldn't make head or tail of it, Jem; could you, my lad?"

"Look there, Grandfather," I said, as I handed him the little piece of paper, and told him how I had got it.

"Well, to be sure!" said my grandfather. "So he gave you this, did he?" and he read aloud:

"On Christ, the solid Rock, I stand,

All other ground is sinking sand."

"Well now, Jem, what does he mean? He kept on saying to me, 'You're on the sand; my friend; you're on the sand, and it won't stand the storm.' What do you make of it,

Jem? Did you hear him, my lad?"

"Yes," said Jem, thoughtfully, "and it has set me thinking, Sandy; I know what he meant well enough."

"And pray what might that be?"

"He meant we can't get to heaven except we come to Christ; we can't get no other way. That's just what it means, Sandy!"

"Do you mean to tell me," said my grandfather, "that I shan't get to heaven if I do my best?"

"No, it won't do, Sandy; there's only one way to heaven; I know that well enough."

"Dear me, Jem!" said my grandfather, "I never heard you talk like that before."

"No," said Jem, "I forgot all about it since I came to the island. I had a good mother years ago; I ought to have done better than I have done."

He said no more, but he was very silent all evening. Grandfather read his newspaper aloud, and talked on all manner of subjects, but Jem Millar's thoughts seemed far away.

The next day was his day for going on

shore. My grandfather and Jem took it in turns, the last Friday in every month. It was the only time they were allowed to leave the island. When it was my grandfather's turn, I generally went with him, and much enjoyed getting a little change. But whichever of them went, it was a great day for us on the island, for they bought any little things that we might be needing for our houses or gardens, and did any business that had to be done on shore.

We all went down to the pier to see Jem Millar set off; and as I was helping him to get on board some empty sacks and some other things he had to take with him, he said to me, in an undertone:

"Alick, my lad, keep that bit of paper; it's all true what that old gentleman said. I've been thinking of it ever since; and, Alick," he whispered, "I believe I *am* on the Rock now."

He said no more, but arranged his oars, and in a minute more he was off. But as he rowed away, I heard him singing softly to himself:

"On Christ, the solid Rock, I stand,
All other ground is sinking sand."

We watched the boat until it was out of sight, and then went home, wishing that it was evening and that Jem was back with all the things we had asked him to get for us.

That was a very gloomy afternoon. A thick fog came over the sea and gradually closed us in, so that we could hardly see a step before us on the beach.

Little Timpey began to cough, so I took her indoors and amused her there with a picture book. It grew so dark that my grandfather lit the lighthouse lamps soon after dinner. There was a dull, yellow light over everything.

I never remember a more gloomy afternoon; and as evening came on, the fog grew denser, till at length we could see nothing outside the windows.

It was no use looking out for Jem's return, for we could not see the sea, much less any boat upon it. So we stayed indoors, and my grandfather sat by the fire smoking his pipe.

"I thought Jem would have been here before now," he said at length, as I was putting out the cups and saucers for tea.

"Oh, he'll come before we've finished tea, I think, Grandfather," I answered. "I wonder what sort of a spade he'll have got for us."

When tea was over, the door opened suddenly, and we looked up, expecting to see Jem enter with our purchases. But it was not Jem, it was his wife.

"Sandy," she said, "what time do you make it? My clock's stopped!"

"Twenty minutes past six," said my grandfather, looking at his watch.

"Past six!" she repeated. "Why, Jem's very late!"

"Yes," said Grandfather; "I'll go down to the pier and have a look out."

But he came back soon, saying it was impossible to see anything; the fog was so thick, he was almost afraid of walking over the pier. "But he's bound to be in at seven," he said (for that was the hour the lighthouse men were required to be on the island again), "so he'll soon be back now."

The clock moved on, and still Jem Millar did not come. I saw Mrs Millar running to her door every now and then with her baby in her arms, to look down the garden path. But no one came.

At last the clock struck seven.

"I never knew him to do such a thing before!" said my grandfather, as he rose to go down to the pier once more.

Waiting for the Boat

Poor Mrs Millar went out of her house, and followed my grandfather down to the pier. I waited indoors with little Timpey, straining my ears to listen for the sound of their footsteps coming back again.

But the clock struck half-past seven, and still no sound was to be heard. I could wait no longer; I wrapped the child in a shawl,

and carried her into the Millars' house and left her under the care of Mrs Millar's little servant. And then I ran down through the thick, smothering fog to the pier.

My grandfather was standing there with Mrs Millar. When I came close to them he was saying, "Cheer up, Mary, my lass. He's all right; he's only waiting till this mist has cleared away a bit. You go home, and I'll tell you as soon as ever I hear his boat coming. Why, you're wet through, woman; you'll get your death of cold!"

Her thin calico dress was soaked with the damp in the air, and she was shivering and looked as white as a sheet. At first she would not be persuaded to leave the pier; but, as

78

time went on, and it grew darker and colder, she consented to do as my grandfather told her, and he promised he would send me up to the lighthouse to tell her as soon as Jem arrived.

When she was gone, my grandfather said, "Alick, there's something wrong with Jem, depend upon it! I didn't like to tell her so, poor soul. If we only had the boat I would go out a bit of a way and see."

We walked up and down the pier, and stopped every now and then to listen if we could hear the sound of oars in the distance, for we should not be able to see the boat till it was close upon us, so dense had the fog become.

"Dear me," my grandfather kept saying, anxiously, "I wish he would come!"

My thoughts went back to the bright sunny morning when Jem Millar had set off, and we had heard him singing, as he went, those two lines of the hymn,

"On Christ, the solid Rock, I stand,
All other ground is sinking sand."

The time passed on. Would he never come? We grew more and more anxious, Mrs Millar's servant-girl came running down to say her mistress wanted to know if we could hear anything yet.

"No," my grandfather said, "nothing yet, my lass; but it can't be long now."

"Missis is so poorly," said the girl; "I think she's got a cold; she shakes all over, and she keeps fretting so."

"Poor soul! Well, perhaps it's better so."

"Whatever do you mean, Grandfather?" I asked.

"Why, if anything is amiss, she won't be so taken aback as if she wasn't afraid; and if Jem's all right she'll only be better pleased."

The girl went back and we still waited on the pier. "Grandfather," I said at length, "I think I hear a boat."

It was a very still night; we stood and listened. At first my grandfather said he heard nothing; but at length he distinguished, as I did, the regular splash – splash – splash – of oars in the distance.

"Yes, it is a boat," said my grandfather.

I was hastening to leave the pier and run up to the house to tell Mrs Millar; but my grandfather laid his hand on my shoulder.

"Wait a bit, Alick, my lad," he said; "let us hear what it is first; maybe it isn't Jem, after all!"

"But it's coming here, Grandfather, I can hear it better now."

"Yes," he said, "it's coming here." But he still kept his hand on my shoulder.

The boat had been a long way off when we first heard it, for it was many minutes before the sound of the oars seemed to become much more distinct. But it came nearer, and nearer, and nearer. Yes, the boat was evidently making for the island.

At last it came so near, that my grandfather called out from the end of the pier,

"Hello, Jem! You're late, my lad!"

"Hello!" said a voice from the boat, but it wasn't Jem's voice. "Whereabouts is your landing place?" said the voice. "It's so thick I can't see."

"Why, Jem isn't there, Grandfather!" I said, catching hold of his arm.

"No," said my grandfather, "I knew there was something wrong with the lad."

He called out to the man in the boat the direction in which he was to row, and then he and I went down the steps together, and waited for the boat to come up.

There were four men in the boat. They were sailors and strangers to me. One of

O. F. Walton

them, the one whose voice we had heard, got out to speak to my grandfather.

"Something's wrong," said my grandfather, before he could begin, "something's wrong with that poor lad."

"Yes," said the man, "we've got him here," and he pointed to the boat.

A cold shudder passed over me as he said this, and I caught sight of something lying at the men's feet at the bottom of the boat.

"What's wrong with him? Has he had an accident? Is he much hurt?"

"He's dead!" said the man, solemnly.

"Oh dear!" said my grandfather, in a choking voice. "However shall we tell his wife? However shall we tell poor Mary?"

"How did it happen?" I asked at length, as soon as I could speak.

"He was getting a sack of flour on board, over yonder," said one of the men in the boat, "and it was awful thick and foggy, and he missed his footing on the plank, and fell in; that's how it happened!"

"Yes," said another man, "and it seems he couldn't swim, and there was no boat nigh at hand to help him. Joe Malcolmson was there and saw him fall in; but before he could call any of us, it was all over with him. We got him out at last, but he was quite gone; we fetched a doctor, and took him into a house nearby, and rubbed him and did all we could; but it was of no good at all! Shall we bring him in?"

"Wait a bit," said my grandfather "we must tell that poor girl first. Which of you will go and tell her?"

The men looked at each other and did not speak. At last one of them, who knew my grandfather a little said, "You'd better tell her, Sandy; she knows you and she'll bear it better than from strangers. We'll wait here till you come back and then we can bring him in."

"Well," said my grandfather with a groan, "I'll go then! Come with me, Alick, my lad," he said, turning to me, "but no, perhaps I'd better go by myself."

So he went very slowly up towards the lighthouse, and I remained behind with the four men on the shore and that silent form lying at the bottom of the boat.

I was much frightened, and felt as if it was all a very terrible dream, and as if I should soon wake up to find it had all passed away.

A Change in the Lighthouse

It seemed a long time before my grandfather came back, and then he only said in a low voice, "You can bring him now, my lads; she knows about it now."

And so the mournful little procession moved on, through the field and garden and courtyard, to the Millars' house, my grandfather and I following.

I shall never forget that night, nor the strange solemn feeling I had then.

Mrs Millar was very ill; the shock had been too much for her. The men went back in the boat to bring a doctor to the island to see her, and the doctor sent them back again to bring a nurse. He said he was afraid she would have an attack of brain-fever, and he thought her very ill indeed.

My grandfather and I sat in the Millars' house all night, for the nurse did not arrive until early in the morning. The six children were fast asleep in their little beds. I went to look at them once, to see if my little Timpey was all right; she was lying in little Polly's bed, their tiny hands fast clasped together as they slept. The tears came fast into my eyes, as I thought that they both had lost a father, and yet neither of them knew anything of their loss!

When the nurse arrived, my grandfather and I went home. But we could not sleep; we lit the kitchen fire, and sat over it in silence for a long time.

Then my grandfather said, "Alick, my lad, it has given me such a turn as I haven't had for many a day. It might have been *me*, Alick; it might just as well have been *me*!"

I put my hand in his, and grasped it very tightly, as he said this. "Yes," he said again, "it might have been me; and if it had, I wonder where I should have been now!"

I didn't speak, and he went on:

"I wonder where Jem is now, poor fellow; I've been thinking of that all night, ever since I saw him lying there at the bottom of that boat."

So I told him of what Jem Millar had said to me the last time I had seen him.

"On the rock!" said my grandfather. "Did he say he was on the rock? Dear me! I wish I could say as much, Alick, my lad."

"Can't you and I come as he came, Grandfather?" I said. "Can't we come and build on the rock, too?"

"Well," said my grandfather, "I wish we could, my lad. I begin to see what he meant, and what the old gentleman meant too. He said, 'You're on the sand, my friend; you're on the sand, and it won't stand the storm; no, it won't stand the storm.' I've just had those words in my ears all the time we were sitting over there by Mrs Millar. But dear me, I don't know how to get on the rock; I don't indeed."

The whole of the next week poor Mrs Millar lay between life and death. At first the doctor gave no hope whatever of her recovery; but after a time she grew a little better, and he began to speak more encouragingly. I spent my time with the poor children, and hardly left them a moment, doing all I could to keep them quietly happy, that they might not disturb their mother.

One sorrowful day only, my grandfather and I were absent for several hours from the lighthouse; we went ashore to follow poor Jem Millar to the grave. His poor wife was unconscious and knew nothing of what was going on.

When, after some weeks, the fever left her, she was still very weak and unfit for

work. But there was much to be done, and she had no time to sit still, for a new man had been appointed to take her husband's place; and he was to come into the house at the beginning of the month.

We felt very dull and sad the day that the Millars went away. We went down to the pier with them and saw them on board the steamer – Mrs Millar, the six little children and the servant girl, all dressed in mourning and all of them crying. They were going to Mrs Millar's home, far away in the north of Scotland where her old father and mother were still living.

The island seemed very lonely and desolate when they were gone. If it had not been for our little sunbeam, as my grandfather called her, I do not know what we should have done. Every day we loved her more, and what we dreaded most was that a letter would arrive some Monday morning to tell us that she must go away from us.

"Dear me, Alick," my grandfather would often say, "how little you and I thought that stormy night what a little treasure we had got wrapped up in that funny little bundle!"

The child was growing fast; the fresh sea air did her great good and every day she became more intelligent and pretty.

We were very curious to know who was appointed in Jem Millar's place; but we were not able to find out even what his name was. Captain Sayers said that he did not know anything about it; and the gentlemen who came over once or twice to see about the house being repaired and put in order for the newcomer were very silent on the subject and seemed to think us very inquisitive if we asked any questions. Of course, our comfort depended very much upon who our neighbour was, for he and my grandfather would be constantly together and we should have no one else to speak to.

My grandfather was very anxious that we should give the man a welcome to the island and make him comfortable on his first arrival. So we set to work, as soon as the Millars were gone, to dig up the untidy garden belonging to the next house and make it as neat and pretty as we could for the newcomers.

"I wonder how many of them there will be," I said, as we were at work in their garden.

"Maybe only just the man," said my grandfather, "When I came here first I was a young unmarried man, Alick. But we shall soon know all about him, he'll be here next Monday morning, they say."

"It's a wonder he hasn't been over before," I said, "to see the house and the island. I wonder what he'll think of it?"

"He'll be strange at first, poor fellow," said my grandfather; "but we'll give him a welcome. Have a nice bit of breakfast for him, Alick, my lad, and for his wife and bairns too, if he has any – hot coffee and cakes and a bit of meat and anything else you like; they'll be glad of it after crossing over here."

So we made our little preparations and waited very anxiously indeed for Monday's steamer.

Our New Neighbour

Monday morning came and found us standing on the pier as usual, awaiting the arrival of the steamer.

We were very anxious indeed to see our new neighbours. A nice little breakfast for four or five people was set out in our little kitchen and I had gathered a large bunch of dahlias from our garden to make the table look cheerful and bright.

p.17 & 86.

All was ready and in due time the steamer came puffing up towards the pier and we saw a man standing on the deck talking to Captain Sayers, who we felt sure must be the new lighthouse man.

"I don't see a wife," said my grandfather.

"Nor any children," said I, as I held little Timpey up that she might see the steamer.

"Puff, puff, puff," she said, as it came up and then turned round and laughed merrily.

The steamer came up to the landing-place and my grandfather and I went down the steps to meet Captain Sayers and the stranger.

"Here's your new neighbour, Sandy," said the captain. "Will you show him the way to his house, whilst I see to your goods?"

"Welcome to the island," said my grandfather, grasping his hand.

He was a tall, strongly built man, very sun-burnt and weather-beaten.

"Thank you," said the man, looking at me all the time. "It is pleasant to have a welcome."

"That's my grandson, Alick," said my grandfather, putting his hand on my shoulder.

"Your grandson," repeated the man,

looking earnestly at me, "your grandson indeed!"

"And now come along," said my grandfather, "and get a bit of something to eat; we've got a cup of coffee all ready for you at home and you'll be right welcome, I assure you."

"That's very kind of you," said the stranger.

We were walking towards the house and the man did not seem much inclined to talk. I fancied once that I saw a tear in his eye, but I thought I must have been mistaken. What could he have to cry about? I little knew all that was passing through his mind.

"By-the-by," said my grandfather, turning round suddenly upon him, "what's your name? We've never heard it yet!"

The man did not answer and my grandfather looked at him in astonishment. "Have you got no name?" he said, "or have you objections to folks knowing what your name is?"

"Father!" said the man, taking hold of

my grandfather's hand, "don't you know your own lad?"

"Why, it's my David! Alick, look Alick, that's your father, it is indeed!"

And then my grandfather fairly broke down and sobbed like a child, whilst my father grasped him tightly with one hand and put the other on my shoulder.

"I wouldn't let them tell you," he said; "I made them promise not to tell you till I could do it myself. I heard of Jem Millar's death as soon as I arrived in England and I wrote off and applied for the place at once. I told them I was your son, Father, and they gave me it at once, as soon as they heard where I had been all these years."

"And where have you been, David, never to send us a line all the time?"

"Well, it's a long story," said my father, "let's come in and I'll tell you all about it."

So we went in together and my father still looked at me. "He's very like *her*, Father," he said in a husky voice.

I knew he meant my mother!

"Then you heard about poor Alice?" said my grandfather.

"Yes," he said, "it was a very curious thing. A man from these parts happened to be on board the vessel I came home in and he told me all about it. I felt as if I had no heart left in me when I heard she was gone. I had just been thinking all the time how glad she would be to see me."

Then my grandfather told him all he could about my poor mother. How she had longed

to hear from him; and how, as week after week and month after month went by, and no news came, she had gradually become weaker and weaker. All this and much more he told him; and whenever he stopped, my father always wanted to hear more, so that it was not until we were sitting over the watch-room fire in the evening that my father began to tell us his story.

He had been shipwrecked on the coast of China. The ship had gone to pieces not far from shore and he and three other men had escaped safely to land. As soon as they stepped on shore, a crowd of Chinese gathered round them with anything but friendly faces. They were taken prisoners and carried before some man who seemed to be the governor of that part of the country. He asked them a great many questions, but they did not understand a word of what he said and, of course, could not answer him.

For some days my father and the other men were very uncertain what their fate would be; for the Chinese at that time were exceedingly jealous of any foreigner landing on their shore. However, one day they were brought out of the wooden house in which they had been imprisoned and taken a long journey of some two hundred miles into the interior of the country. And here it was that my poor father had been all those years, when we thought him dead. He was not unkindly treated and he taught the half-civilised people there many things which they did not know and which they were very glad to learn. But both by day and night he was carefully watched lest he should make his escape and he never found a single opportunity of getting away from them. Of course, there was no postal service and no railways in that remote place, and he was quite shut out from the world. Of what was going on at home he knew as little as if he had been living on the moon.

Slowly and drearily eleven long years passed away, and then, one morning, they were suddenly told that they were to be sent down to the coast and put on board a ship bound for England. They told my father that there had been a war and that one of the conditions of peace was that they should give up all the foreigners in their country, whom they were holding as prisoners.

"Well, David, my lad," said my grandfather, when he had finished his strange story, "it's almost like getting thee back from the dead, to have thee in the old home again!"

On the Rock

About a fortnight after my father arrived, we were surprised one Monday morning by another visit from old Mr Davis. His son-in-law had asked him to come to tell my grandfather that he had received a letter with regard to the little girl who was saved from the *Victory*. So he told my father and me as we stood on the pier; and all the way to the house I was wondering what the letter could be.

Timpey was running by my side, her little hand in mine, and I could not bear to think how dull we should be when she was gone.

"Why, it's Mr Davis," said my grandfather, as he rose to meet the old gentleman.

"Yes," said he, "it is Mr Davis; and I suppose you can guess what I've come for."

"Not to take our little sunbeam, sir," said my grandfather, taking Timpey in his arms. "You never mean to say you're going to take her away?"

"Wait a bit," said the old gentleman, sitting down and fumbling in his pocket; "wait until you've heard this letter and then see what you think about her going."

And he began to read as follows:

"My Dear Sir, - I am almost overpowered with joy by the news received by telegram an hour ago. We had heard of the loss of the Victory, and were mourning for our little darling as being amongst the number of those

Lighthouse Keeper
Alexander Ferguson
Rinslie Craig Lighthouse

drowned. Her mother has been quite crushed by her loss and has been dangerously ill ever since the sad intelligence reached us.

"Need I tell you what our feelings were, when we suddenly heard that our dear child was alive, well and happy!

"We shall sail by the next steamer for England to claim our little darling. My wife is hardly strong enough to travel this week or we should come at once. A thousand thanks to the brave men who saved our little girl. I shall hope soon to be able to thank them myself. My heart is too full to write much today.

"Our child was travelling home under the care of a friend, as we wished her to leave India before the hot weather set in and I was not able to leave for two months. This accounts for the name Villiers not being on the list of passengers on board the Victory. Thank you most sincerely for all your efforts to let us know of our child's safety.

"I remain, yours very truly,
     Edward Villiers."

"Now," said the old gentleman, looking at me and laughing, though I saw a tear in his eye, "won't you let them have her?"

"Well, to be sure," said my grandfather, "what can one say after that? Poor things, how pleased they are!"

"Timpey," I said, taking the little girl on my knee, "who do you think is coming to see you? Your mother is coming – coming to see little Timpey!"

The child looked earnestly at me; she evidently had not quite forgotten the name. She opened her blue eyes wider than usual, and looked very thoughtful for a minute or two. Then she nodded her head very wisely and said,

"Dear mother coming to see Timpey?"

"Bless her!" said the old gentleman, stroking her fair little head, "she seems to know all about it."

Then we sat down to breakfast; and whilst we were eating it, old Mr Davis turned to me and asked if I had read the little piece of paper he had given me on his last visit.

O. F. Walton

"Yes, sir," said my grandfather, "indeed we have read it," and he told him about Jem Millar and what he had said to me that last morning.

"And now," said my grandfather, "I wish, if you'd be so kind, you would tell me *how to get on the rock*, for I'm on the sand now; there's no doubt at all about it, and I'm afraid, as you said the last time you were here, that it won't stand the storm."

"It would be a sad thing," said old Mr Davis, "to be on the sand when the Great Storm comes."

"Ay, sir, it would be," said my grandfather, "I often lie in bed at nights and think of it, when the winds and the waves are raging. I call to mind that verse where it says about the sea and the waves roaring, and men's hearts failing them for fear. Deary me, I should be terrible frightened, that I should, if that day was to come and I saw the Lord coming in glory."

"But you need not be afraid if you are on the Rock," said our old friend. "All who have

come to Christ and are resting on Him will feel as safe in that day as you do when there is a storm raging and you are inside this house."

"Yes," said my grandfather, "I see that sir, but somehow I don't know what you mean by getting on the rock, sir."

"Well," said Mr Davis, "what would you do if this house was built on the sand down there by the shore and you knew that the very first storm that came would sweep it away?"

"Do, sir!" said my grandfather, "why, I should pull it down every stone of it, and build it upon the rock instead."

"Exactly!" said Mr Davis. "You have been building your hopes of heaven on the sand – on your good deeds, on your good intentions, on all sorts of sand-heaps. You know you have."

"Yes," said grandfather, "I know I have."

"Well, my friend," said Mr Davis, "pull them all down. Say to yourself, 'I'm a lost man if I remain as I am; my hopes are all resting on the sand.' And then, build your hopes on something better, something which *will* stand the storm; build them on Christ. He is the only way to heaven. He died that you, a poor sinner, might go there. Build your hopes on Him, my friend. Trust to what He has done for you, as your only hope of heaven – *that* is building on the Rock!"

"I see, sir; I understand you now."

"Do that," said Mr Davis, "and then your hope will be a sure and steadfast hope, a good hope which can never be moved. And when the last great storm comes, it will not touch you, you will be as certainly and as entirely safe in that day as you are in the lighthouse when the storm is raging outside, because you will be built upon the immoveable Rock."

I cannot recollect all the conversation which Mr Davis and my grandfather had that morning, but I do remember that before he went away he knelt down with us and prayed that we might every one of us be found on the Rock, in that last great storm.

And I remember also that, that night, when my grandfather said good-night to me, he said, "Alick, my lad, I don't mean to go to sleep tonight till I can say, like poor Jem Millar, 'On Christ, the solid Rock, I stand,

All other ground is sinking sand.'

And I believe that my grandfather kept his word.

O. F. Walton

The Sunbeam Claimed

It was a cold, cheerless morning; the wind was blowing and the rain was beating against the windows. It was far too wet and stormy for little Timpey to be out, so she and I had a game of ball together in the kitchen, whilst my father and grandfather went down to the pier.

She looked such a pretty little thing that morning. She had on a little blue frock, which Mrs Millar had made for her out of the material my grandfather had bought, and a clean white pinafore. She was screaming with delight as I threw the ball over her head and she ran to catch it - when the door opened, and my father ran in.

"Alick, is she here? They've come!"

"Who've come, Father?" I said.

"Little Timpey's father and mother; they are coming up the garden now with your grandfather!"

He had hardly finished speaking before my grandfather came in with a lady and a gentleman. The lady ran forward as soon as she saw her child, put her arms round her and held her tightly, as if she could never part from her again. Then she sat down with the little darling on her knee, stroking her tiny hands and talking to her and looking, oh, so anxiously, to see if the child remembered her.

At first, Timpey looked a little shy and

hung down her head and would not look in her mother's face. But this was only for a minute. As soon as her mother spoke to her she evidently remembered her voice and when Mrs Villiers asked her, with tears in her eyes, "Do you know me, little Timpey? My dear little Timpey, who am I?" the child looked up and smiled, as she said, "Dear mother – Timpey's dear mother!" and she put up her little fat hand to stroke her mother's face.

And then, when I saw that, I could feel no longer sorry that the child was going away.

I can well remember what a happy morning that was. Mr and Mrs Villiers were so kind to us and so very grateful for all that my grandfather and I had done for their little girl. They thought her looking so much better and stronger than when she left India, and they were so pleased to find that she had not forgotten all the little lessons she had learnt at home. Mrs Villiers seemed as if she could not take her eyes off the child; wherever little Timpey went and whatever she was doing, her mother followed her and I shall never forget how happy and how glad both the father and the mother looked.

But the most pleasant day will come to an end; and in the evening a boat was to come from shore to take Mr and Mrs Villiers and their child away.

"Dear me!" said my grandfather, with a groan, as he took the little girl on his knee, "I never felt so sorry to lose anybody, *never*, I'm sure I didn't. Why, I calls her my little sunbeam, sir! You'll excuse me saying so, but I don't feel over and above kindly to you for taking her away from me; I don't indeed, sir."

"Then I don't know what you will say to me, when you hear I want to rob you further," said Mr Villiers.

"Rob me further?" repeated my grandfather.

"Yes," said Mr Villiers, putting his hand on my shoulder. "I want to take this grandson of yours away too. It seems to me a great pity that such a fine lad should waste his days shut up on this little island. Let him come with me and I will send him to a really good school for three or four years and then I will get him some good clerkship, or something of that kind, and put him in the way of making his way in the world. Now then, my friend, will you and his father spare him?"

"Well," said my grandfather, "I don't know what to say to you, sir; it's very good of you, very good indeed it is, and it would be a fine thing for Alick, it would indeed; but I always thought he would take my place here when I was dead."

"Yes," said my father, "but you see *I* shall be here to do that, father; and if Mr Villiers is so very kind as to take Alick, I'm sure we ought only to be too glad for him to have such a friend."

"You're right, David, yes, you're right. We mustn't be selfish, sir, and you'd let him come and see us sometimes, wouldn't you?"

"Oh, to be sure," said Mr Villiers, "he can come and spend his holidays here and give you fine histories of his school life. Now Alick, what say you? There's an excellent school in the town where we are going to live, so you would be near us and you could come to see us on holiday afternoons and see whether Timpey remembers all you have taught her. What say you?"

I was very pleased indeed, and thankful for his kindness. My father and grandfather said they would never be able to repay him.

"Repay *me!*" said Mr Villiers. "Why my friends, it's *I* who can never repay *you*. Just think, for one moment, of what you have given me," and he put his arm round his little girl's neck. "So we may consider that matter settled. And now, when can Alick come?"

My grandfather begged for another month and Mr Villiers said that would do very well, as in that time the school would reopen after the holidays. And so it came to pass, that when I said good-bye to little Timpey that afternoon, it was with the hope of soon seeing her again.

Her father called her Lucy, which I found was her real name. Timpey was a pet name, which had been given her as a baby. But though Lucy was certainly a prettier name, still I felt I should always think of her as Timpey – *my* little Timpey.

I shall never forget my feelings that month. A strange new life was opening out before me and I felt quite bewildered by the prospect.

My grandfather and father and I sat over the watch-room fire, night after night, talking over my future; and day after day I wandered over our dear little island, wondering how I should feel when I said good-bye to it, and went into the great world beyond.

Since old Mr Davis' visit there had been a great change in our little home. The great Bible had been taken down from its place and carefully read and studied, and Sunday was no longer spent by us like any other day, but was kept as well as it could be on that lonely island.

My grandfather, I felt sure, was a new man. Old things had passed away, all things had become new. He was dearer to me than ever, and I felt very sorrowful when I thought of parting from him.

"I could never have left you, Grandfather," I said one day, "if my father had not been here."

"No," he said, "I don't think I could have spared you, Alick; but your father just came back at the right time; didn't you David?"

At last the day arrived on which Mr Villiers had appointed to meet me at the town to which the steamer went every Monday morning, when it left the island. My father and grandfather walked with me down to the pier and saw me on board. And the very last thing my grandfather said to me was, "Alick, my lad, keep on the Rock; be sure you keep on the Rock!"

And I trust that I have never forgotten my grandfather's last words to me.

It was founded upon a rock.
Matthew 7:25

My hope is built on nothing less
Than Jesus' blood and righteousness;
I dare not trust the sweetest frame,
But wholly lean on Jesus' name,
On Christ, the solid Rock, I stand,
All other ground is sinking sand.

When long appears my toilsome race,
I rest on His unchanging grace;
In every high and stormy gale,
My anchor holds within the veil
On Christ the solid Rock, I stand,
All other ground is sinking sand.

His oath, His covenant and blood,
Support me in the whelming flood;
When every earthly prop gives way,
He then is all my hope and stay.
On Christ the solid Rock, I stand,
All other ground is sinking sand.

When the last trumpet's voice shall sound,
Oh, may I then in Him be found;
Robed in His righteousness alone,
Faultless to stand before the throne.
On Christ the solid Rock, I stand,
All other ground is sinking sand.

MOTE

Jesus' blood and righteousness

The line of the hymn goes:
*My hope is built on nothing less than
Jesus' blood and righteousness.*
What does this mean? If you read the gospels, in particular Matthew chapters 26-28; Mark chapters 14-16; Luke chapters 22-24 and John chapters 18-21 you will read about Jesus' death and resurrection. This is what our hope is built on and we are hoping for forgiveness of sins, eternal life, a never ending life with Jesus in heaven when we die.

This is not an uncertain hope. When we hope in Jesus we are absolutely certain that what he promised will come true. We are promised forgiveness of sins through Christ's death for us. How could his death achieve this? It is because of his righteousness; his perfection. Christ has never and will never do anything wrong or sinful. When Christ died on the cross he took our punishment and because he was sinless, Christ's perfect sacrifice has purchased, in an amazing and wonderful way, eternal life for all who believe in his name.

Bible Verse: *1 Peter 1:3-5 (NKJ)*

Wholly lean on Jesus' name.

I dare not trust the sweetest frame,
But wholly lean on Jesus' name.
What is it about the name of Jesus that is so wonderful? The name Jesus means - God saves.

What does God save us from? God saves us from sin, from the devil and from eternal punishment. It is because of God's love that we are rescued. *For God so loved the world that he gave his only begotten Son, that whoever believes in him should not perish but have everlasting life. John 3:16.*

Jesus has many wonderful names. He is the Way, the Truth and the Life - which tell us that he is the only one we should trust for eternal salvation. The Son of God shows us that he is God and that he is divine; the Lamb of God shows us that he willingly sacrificed his life to save us from our sins. The name Christ tells us that he is God's chosen one, that he is the only one who can bring us back to a full relationship with God.

With all these wonderful names we can only trust in Jesus, there is no other who has the words of eternal life. Trust in him completely

Bible Verse: *Acts 4:12 (NKJ)*

My anchor holds within the veil

The next verse of the hymn mentions races and stormy gales:

When long appears my toilsome race,
I rest on His unchanging grace;
In every high and stormy gale,
My anchor holds within the veil.

Life is like a race sometimes. People try to be first or the most important. But the Christian race is different. We should live our lives not for ourselves, but for Christ. Living as a Christian can be a hard struggle. But when things get difficult we can rely on Jesus. He is always loving and merciful.

If you've ever been in a storm at sea you will know how scary it is. Ships can be tossed about by the waves. They can even be cast up on the rocks and smashed to pieces if they aren't held secure by a strong anchor.

If you don't trust in Jesus, life can be like a dangerous storm. Sin and temptations can make you do things which not only destroy your life but take you away from God. Those who believe and follow Christ are like boats with strong anchors. The word of God tells us how to live, and the love and forgiveness of Christ keeps us safe for all time and eternity.

Bible Verse: Hebrews 6:19 (NKJ)

His oath, His covenant and blood

What does the word oath mean?

His oath, His covenant, and blood,
Support me in the whelming flood.

An oath is another word for a promise. A covenant is an important promise which cannot be broken. God has made a covenant with his people - with all who believe in the name of his Son, Jesus Christ. Because Jesus took our punishment on the cross, God looks on those who believe in Jesus and sees Jesus' righteousness instead of their sin.

Throughout the Bible, God promised his people that sin would be dealt with. He promised a redeemer - but he also promised judgement for those who rejected him and followed a life of sin. God has promised salvation - and this has been achieved through the death of Jesus Christ.

God's word is flawless and just, his promises are kept forever and never broken. Christ's blood is pure and powerful and, when death comes, it is only the fact that Jesus died for us that will bring us safely through death to eternal life.

Bible Verse: *John 3:16 (NKJ)*

He then is all my hope and stay.

The next verse of the hymn tells us about who we should trust:

When every earthly prop gives way,
He then is all my hope and stay.

We can sometimes place our hope on things which don't deserve it like money or good exam results? It is good to pass exams and to have a job and we should thank God for these. God can bless us in many different ways. But putting all your hope in something other than Jesus Christ is disasterous.

If you are putting your trust in things - then what happens when these things are destroyed? Your hope is destroyed. What happens when the people you love die? Your hope dies with them. In the end things, money, exams and even people don't last forever. These are earthly things. The Bible tells us to set our hope on things above, not on earthly things. Earthly things fall apart eventually, they aren't built to last.

Just as a building needs good foundations - our lives need foundations for today and for eternity. Jesus Christ is the only lasting strong foundation for us to rely on. He is the rock.

Bible Verse: *1 Corinthians 3:11 (NKJ)*

When the last trumpet's voice shall sound

What does this verse means?

When the last trumpet's voice shall sound,
Oh, may I then in Him be found;

Today when you hear a trumpet it's usually in an orchestra, but in the past trumpets would announce the beginning of a battle or tell everyone that the king was making an appearance.

One day, Jesus Christ will return. When he first came to earth he arrived as a baby in a stable, but when Jesus comes back he is going to come as a victorious King. The bodies of those who loved him will rise from their graves as he did. They will be reunited with their souls and ushered into the eternal kingdom to live forever with their Saviour.

Those who did not follow Jesus will face a different eternal future - one of weeping and wailing and separation in hell. Come to Jesus now and when that moment arrives you will be found in him. Eternal life and not death will be a reality for you.

Bible Verse: *1 Thessalonians 4:15-17 (NKJ)*

Robed in His righteousness alone,

What does it mean to be robed in righteousness?

Robed in His righteousness alone,
Faultless to stand before the throne.

There is a story in the Bible about someone who turned up at a wedding unsuitably dressed. He was thrown out. Jesus used this story to illustrate that, on the last day, we must be ready. If you aren't covered by Jesus' righteousness you are not ready for eternity. Some people think that to get to heaven they must be good and decent. But it's a lot more than that.

If you go through life just being nice, you still won't be good enough for heaven. There is only one way to be ready to meet with God and that is to meet with Jesus before you die. Instead of relying on what you have done, you rely on what Jesus did. His death means that you can stand before God clothed in Jesus' perfect righteousness.

On the last day when we meet God, if we belong to Christ we will be like him - faultless and perfect.

Bible Verse: *2 Corinthians 5:21 (NKJ)*

On Christ the solid Rock, I stand, All other ground is sinking sand.

If you are walking along an unknown beach be careful where you walk. Beaches can be lonely places and dangerous. One danger is sinking sand. This is sand that isn't firm to walk on like normal sand, and if you stand on it you can start to sink. It is very difficult to get out of - the more you struggle the harder it gets to pull your feet out to safety.

The other things that you will notice on a beach are the rocks and rock pools. A rock is hard and firm and isn't like sinking sand at all. It is the opposite. So why is Jesus Christ like a rock and everything else like sinking sand?

When you die or when Jesus returns, there are only two options - eternal life or eternal death. If you are safe with Christ you are standing on solid ground - there is no danger. Eternal life is yours. If you are not then you are on dangerous ground. All other religions are false. If you don't trust Christ then eternal life is not yours. You are on sinking sand. Get to safety while you still can - ask God to forgive your sin in Jesus' name.

Bible Verse: *Matthew 7:24-25 (NKJ)*

Classic

Fiction

CHRISTIE'S OLD ORGAN

By O F Walton

Christie knows what it is like to be homeless and on the streets - that's why he is overjoyed to be given a roof over his head by Old Treffy, the Organ Grinder. But Treffy is old and sick and Christie is worried about him. All that Treffy wants is to have peace in his heart and a home of his own. That is what Christie wants too. Christie hears about how Heaven is like *Home Sweet Home*. Everytime he plays it on Treffy's barrel organ he wonders if he and Treffy can find their way to God's special home. Find out how God uses Christie and the old barrel organ and lots of friends along the way to bring Treffy and Christie to their own *Home Sweet Home*.

ISBN 1-8579-2523-8

Classic
Fiction

A PEEP BEHIND THE SCENES

By O F Walton

Rosalie and her mother are tired of living a life with no home and precious little hope. But Rosalie's father runs a travelling theatre company and they are forced to travel from one town to the next, year in year out. Rosalie's father has no objections but Rosalie's mother remembers a better life, before she was married, when she had parents who loved her and a sister to play with. Through her memories Rosalie is introduced to the family she never knew she had. Rosalie and her mother are also introduced to somebody else - The Good Shepherd. They hear for the first time about the God who loves them. Rosalie rejoices to hear about a real home in Heaven but will she finally find this other home that she has heard about - or is it too late? Will God help her find her family? Of course he will!

ISBN 1-8579-2524-6

START COLLECTING NOW

Ten Boys who changed the World

Would you like to change your world? These ten boys grew up to do just that:

Billy Graham, Brother Andrew, John Newton, George Müller, Nicky Cruz, William Carey, David Livingstone, Adoniram Judson, Eric Liddell, Luis Palau.

Find out how Eric won the race and honoured God; David became an explorer and explained the Bible; Nicky joined the gangs and then the church; Andrew smuggled Bibles into Russia and brought hope to thousands and John captured slaves but God used him to set them free.

Find out what God wants you to do!

ISBN: 1-85792-579-3

LIGHT KEEPERS

START COLLECTING NOW

Ten Girls who changed the World

Would you like to change your world? These ten girls grew up to do just that:

Isobel Kuhn, Elizabeth Fry, Amy Carmichael, Gladys Aylward, Mary Slessor, Catherine Booth, Jackie Pullinger, Evelyn Brand, Joni Eareckson Tada, Corrie Ten Boom.

Find out how Corrie saved lives and loved Jesus in World War II; Mary saved babies in Africa and fought sin; Gladys rescued 100 children and trusted God; Joni survived a crippling accident and still thanked Jesus; Amy rescued orphans and never gave up; Isobel taught the Lisu about Christ and followed him; Evelyn obeyed God in India and taught others too; Jackie showed love in awful conditions in Hong Kong; Elizabeth followed Christ and won justice and Catherine rolled up her sleeves and helped the homeless!

Find out what God wants you to do!

ISBN: 1-85792-649-8

TRAIL BLAZERS

Mary Slessor
Servant to the Slave

by Catherine Mackenzie

Mary Slessor had no advantages in life, she was a rough, tough, street urchin... but that was what God needed. Find out how a scruffy little girl from a poor family became one of the most respected white women in Africa.

God chose Mary Slessor because the Africans needed someone to respect them and get alongside them. Mary brought good news to Africa... the good news of health and education for all, respect for women and most importantly the love of God to all men - black or white.

ISBN: 1-85792-348-0

Children's Stories

by J C Ryle

John Charles Ryle was born at Macclesfield in the north of England in 1816. The son of a wealthy banker, he was educated at Eton and Oxford University and was destined for a career in politics. Ryle was also a fine athlete who rowed and played cricket for Oxford.

As a result of hearing Ephesians chapter 2 read at church, Ryle became a Christian at the age of twenty-two and was ordained four years later, in 1842. He then ministered in several country churches before being appointed as the first Bishop of Liverpool in 1880.

Ryle was a well-known writer of many tracts and books as well as a faithful pastor. Children loved and looked up to him. This book is a compilation of the stories he read to the children in his congregation.

ISBN: 1-85792-639-0

CHRISTIAN FOCUS

Staying faithful! Reaching out!

Christian Focus Publications publishes biblically-accurate books for adults and children under its three main imprints: Christian Focus; Mentor and Christian Heritage.

Our children's publication list includes a Sunday school curriculum which covers pre-school to early teens; puzzle and activity books; personal and family devotional titles as well as biography and inspirational stories that children will love.

If you are looking for quality Bible teaching for children then we have a wide and excellent range of Bible story books - from board books to teenage fiction, we have it covered.

These children's books are bright, fun and full of biblical truth. At Christian Focus it is our aim to help children find out about God and get them enthusiastic about reading the Bible, now and later in their lives.

Find us at our web page:
www.christianfocus.com